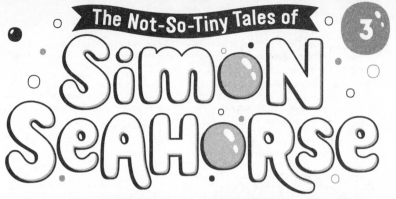

The Not-So-Tiny Tales of Simon Seahorse

3

Don't Pop the Bubble Ball!

By Cora Reef
Illustrated by Liam Darcy

LITTLE SIMON

New York   London   Toronto   Sydney   New Delhi

LITTLE SIMON

An imprint of Simon & Schuster Children's Publishing Division

1230 Avenue of the Americas, New York, New York 10020

First Little Simon paperback edition December 2021

Copyright © 2021 by Simon & Schuster, Inc.

All rights reserved, including the right of reproduction in whole or in part in any form.

LITTLE SIMON is a registered trademark of Simon & Schuster, Inc., and associated colophon is a trademark of Simon & Schuster, Inc. For information about special discounts for bulk purchases, please contact Simon & Schuster Special Sales at 1-866-506-1949 or business@simonandschuster.com.

The Simon & Schuster Speakers Bureau can bring authors to your live event. For more information or to book an event contact the Simon & Schuster Speakers Bureau at 1-866-248-3049 or visit our website at www.simonspeakers.com.

Designed by Leslie Mechanic

The text of this book was set in Causten Round.

Manufactured in the United States of America 1121 MTN

10 9 8 7 6 5 4 3 2 1

Library of Congress Cataloging-in-Publication Data

Names: Reef, Cora, author. | Darcy, Liam, illustrator.

Title: Don't pop the bubble ball! / by Cora Reef ; illustrated by Liam Darcy.

Other titles: Do not pop the bubble ball!

Description: First Little Simon paperback edition. | New York : Little Simon, 2021. | Series: The not-so-tiny tales of Simon Seahorse ; 3 | Audience: Ages 5-9. | Audience: Grades K-1. | Summary: Simon and his older sister try out for the bubble ball team together, but they end up on opposing sides.

Identifiers: LCCN 2021044332 (print) | LCCN 2021044333 (ebook) | ISBN 9781665903738 (paperback) | ISBN 9781665903745 (hardcover) | ISBN 9781665903752 (ebook)

Subjects: CYAC: Sea horses—Fiction. | Brothers and sisters—Fiction. | Sports—Fiction.

Classification: LCC PZ7.1.R4423 Do 2021 (print) | LCC PZ7.1.R4423 (ebook) | DDC [Fic]—dc23

LC record available at https://lccn.loc.gov/2021044332

LC ebook record available at https://lccn.loc.gov/2021044333

Contents

Bubble Ball Dreams

"You won't believe what happened today!" Simon Seahorse said as he unpacked his backpack after school.

"Did you meet another shark?" his younger brother, Earl, asked.

"Did you lose your lucky pearl again?" his little sister, Lulu, wanted to know.

A few of Simon's older siblings glanced over from the kitchen table. Simon was one of twelve brothers and sisters, so he always had an audience.

"Close!" Simon said with a laugh.

But just as he was about to launch into one of his incredible tales, his oldest sister, Kya, burst into the house. She was out of breath, and her favorite Deep-Sea Divers cap hung sideways off her head.

"Wow, and I thought I knew how to make an entrance," Simon joked. "Were you being chased by a tiger shark? Or an octopus with eight legs *and* eight heads?"

Kya grinned. "Even better," she said. "I just found out bubble ball tryouts are this weekend!"

"That's great, Kya," Mr. Seahorse said. A few of Simon's siblings nodded in agreement, but no one seemed as excited as Kya. They were all busy with homework or other projects.

Kya's face fell. "Doesn't anyone *care*?" she asked.

"I care!" Simon called

out. He wasn't sure he *really* cared about the tryouts, but he knew Kya did. She'd been eagerly waiting for the season to start up again.

There were two bubble ball teams in Coral Grove: the Tidal Waves and the Deep-Sea Divers. Simon always enjoyed watching Kya play for the Divers—even if he didn't totally understand the rules of the game.

"You should try out too, Simon!"
Kya said. "It would be so fun if we
were on the same team."

"Oh, I don't know. . . ." Simon had
never been very good at sports. He
was smaller than a lot of the other sea
creatures. But, really, he preferred a
good adventure story to a game of tag.

Sometimes while his friends played games on the playground at school, he would swim to the top of the sandcastle. Up there, it was as if he could see the whole ocean. That always inspired him to dream up new stories to tell.

"I could help you get ready for the tryouts," Kya offered.

Simon smiled. "I'll think about it," he told his sister.

As he hopped into bed that night, Simon pictured himself in a bubble ball match. In his imagination, he was a total superstar. He whizzed around all the other players, doing

backflips, dribbling the bubble ball, and spinning it on his tail. He even scored the winning goal of the game!

Of course, he knew that was all just pretend. Still, as he drifted off to sleep, Simon wondered if maybe he really should try out. Tomorrow he'd see what his best friend, Olive Octopus, thought about it. She always had good advice.

Tag,
You're It!

Simon and Olive usually rode the current to school together. But that morning Olive had to stop by the town library with her mom first, so Simon headed to school alone.

As other creatures hopped on and off the current, Simon tried to imagine where they were going.

It was one of his favorite ways to pass the time. A brightly colored parrotfish hopped out at a stop that was near Coral Jungle, and Simon remembered when he and Olive had met Zelda the shark there. Maybe the parrotfish was in for a surprise and would find Zelda there, picking coral flowers again!

When Simon reached Coral Grove Elementary, he swam to the top of the reef to meet Olive. She was working on her juggling skills.

"Hey, Simon!" Olive called, tossing her juggling shells into her backpack one by one.

"Hi, Olive! Guess what?" Simon said.

"Hmm, let me think." Olive scratched her chin. "You got caught in a sandstorm that blew you all the way to the Kelp Forest and then a manta ray swam you to school?"

Simon laughed and shook his head. "No, but that was a good one!"

Olive probably heard more of Simon's stories than anyone else, and she always listened attentively. Sometimes, if he got carried away, she had to remind him that he was just telling a *story*. So he was glad when she added some flair!

"It's about bubble ball tryouts this weekend," Simon continued.

As they swam into Mrs. Tuttle's classroom, Simon told Olive what Kya had said about helping him prepare. "Maybe I really should try out?"

"Ohh, that *would* be fun if you were on the same team as Kya," Olive said.

"You could try out too," Simon said as they found their seats. "I bet you'd be great at bubble ball!"

Olive shook her head. "I can't. I'm helping my mom out with a project at the library. But I'll definitely come cheer you on!"

Simon nodded. "Okay, I'll keep thinking about it."

If nothing else, he was bound to get a good story out of it!

At recess that day, an eel named Nix slithered over to Olive and Simon. "Want to play tag?" she asked.

"Sure!" Simon said. He and Olive hadn't played last time, and tag might give him some good practice for bubble ball ... *if* he was going to try out.

As Nix rounded up the players, Simon found himself next to Cam, the crabbiest student in their class. Cam was a crab, after all.

"Wait, *Olive* is playing? That's not fair," Cam complained. "She has more arms than anyone else."

"What about your claws?" Olive shot back. "They can tag easier than my arms. And Lionel can swim faster than all of us."

"Olive's right. We all have our talents," Simon said. Even if he wasn't sure what *his* were.

"Fine, let's play," Cam grumbled. Then he cried "Simon, you're it!" and scuttled away.

Simon tried to swim after his friends. But no matter how hard he flapped his fins, he wasn't fast enough to catch anyone.

By the end of recess, Simon was panting hard. If he had this much trouble playing tag, how would he ever make the bubble ball team?

Playing by the Rules

When Simon got home from school that afternoon, Kya was out front waiting for him.

"Are you ready for practice?" she asked, spinning a bubble ball on her fin.

Simon didn't realize they'd be jumping *right* into it, and truthfully he wasn't really up for another sport after his performance during tag earlier. But Kya looked so excited. So Simon managed a smile and said "sure!"

"First, let's go over the rules of the game." Kya said. Using a stick, she drew a map of the field in the sand. "This is the ground field," she explained, "but in bubble ball, we don't just play on the ground."

Ah, Simon thought. *That explains why you can't always see the players.*

"The nets on the ground are goals," Kya said, adding to her drawing. "But there are goals in different areas around the field too."

"Are those treasure chests?" Simon asked as Kya drew squares on the edges of the field. "Do we get what's inside if we win the game?"

Kya laughed. "No, those are the bubble ball tanks. They're always making new bubbles."

"Do the bubbles ever get stuck together and turn into a giant bubble monster?" Simon asked.

"No, Simon." Kya rolled her eyes and went on. "The point of the game is to score as many goals as you can, but you're also trying to pop the other team's bubble balls so that they *can't* score."

"What if a school of swordfish swims through the game and they pop all the balls at the same time?" Simon asked.

Kya smiled. "Then both teams would rush to get new balls and keep playing. Okay, ready to practice?"

"Yes!" Simon said. Now that he understood the rules, he *was* actually excited to get started.

After Kya set up a couple of goals, she brought out a bag of bubble balls. She and Simon faced each other, each holding a ball.

Kya whistled and swam right toward Simon. She then spun past him so quickly that he couldn't even see what was happening. Before he knew it, Kya had scored a goal.

"Wow! How did you do that?" Simon cried.

"Practice," Kya said happily. "Now, let me show you how to use your tail to block. That's one good thing about being a seahorse."

Simon nodded. The next time Kya whistled, Simon swam up to try to block her with his tail. But Kya flipped around, popped his bubble ball, and scored again.

"Remember, we can move in any direction we want," Kya said.

The next round, Simon tried to mirror Kya—and he managed to block her! Seeing his chance, he shot his ball around her and scored a goal.

"Great job, Simon!" Kya said. "I just know you'll make the Deep-Sea Divers with me. And then we'll have the best team in Coral Grove!"

Simon's Sport

Kya and Simon continued to practice all week. Simon was surprised at how good he was getting. Not only did his tail make it easier to block, but being small meant he could spin quickly and weave around obstacles. Plus, thanks to his light touch, he rarely popped the ball.

He'd always thought being a seahorse prevented him from being really good at sports, but maybe the sports they played at school just had never been his thing!

One day, Simon brought some bubble balls to the playground so he could teach his friends to play.

Everyone was excited to try it out.

But when they started playing, things didn't go well. Lionel kept forgetting the rules. Cam kept accidentally moving sideways and crashing into Nix. And Olive couldn't seem to hold a bubble ball without popping it.

"You'll get better with practice," Simon assured them. "Keep trying!"

But soon enough Olive had popped the last of the bubble balls and the game was over.

"Oh good," Cam said. "Now we can play tag."

Nix and Lionel looked relieved too.

Even Olive admitted that tag was easier. "But thanks for trying to teach us, Simon," she said. "I'm glad you've found your sport."

Simon smiled. Olive was right. He *had* found his sport. Now he couldn't wait for tryouts!

A few days later, it was finally time!
At home, Simon put on his sweatband
to keep his vision clear. Then he met
Kya downstairs.

"Ready?" she asked.

Simon's stomach fluttered with excitement. "Let's go!"

When they arrived at Seagrass Fields, Simon stopped and stared. He was in awe.

Simon was used to being in the stands, watching the players far below—or above. But now that he was actually out on the field, he couldn't

believe how different everything looked. The stands seemed a lot bigger and the field much longer and the other players a whole lot faster.

Suddenly the excited fluttering in Simon's stomach turned into nervous swirling.

Kya must have been able to tell how he was feeling because she said, "Don't worry, Simon. You've been practicing all week. You'll be great."

Simon tried to smile. "Thanks."

"And if you don't make the team, we can still go out for kelp ice cream after tryouts," Kya added. "Deal?"

Simon's face lit up. "Kelp ice cream? Deal!"

Team Tryouts!

Just as tryouts were about to start, Simon noticed a crab on the field who looked sort of like Cam. Then he spotted Cam himself near the stands. Cam scuttled over to Simon.

"My sister, Cleo, is trying out," he explained.

"I hope she makes it!" Simon said.

Cam nodded and then quietly mumbled something that *almost* sounded like "good luck." Almost.

"Thanks!" Simon called after Cam as he scurried away.

Tweet! One of the coaches had blown a whistle, which meant that tryouts were beginning!

First up was an obstacle course. Everyone would have to go through the course without popping their bubble ball. When it was Simon's turn, he carefully cradled the ball in his tail. He managed to get through the whole course with his bubble ball intact!

Some of the other bubbles popped, but when that happened, the sea creatures were just given a new bubble and allowed to start over.

The second test was for speed. They were timed to see how fast they could swim to the other end of the field. Simon was smaller than a lot of the other players, but he twisted and spun the way Kya had shown him.

He certainly wasn't the fastest, but he managed to get to the other end of the field with a good time. He was really impressed by an eel who slithered so quickly that she was just a blur zipping down the field.

The final test was a scrimmage. They were broken up into two teams so they could play against each other. Simon was on the same team as Cam's sister, Cleo. They played well, but with Kya on the other team, they didn't stand a chance. Kya's team won 4–1.

"Good work, everyone!" one of the coaches said. "We'll post the team lists very soon. Anyone who didn't make it will still be an alternate."

The coach also said that their first match would be next weekend.

That won't give us much time to practice, Simon thought. But then he stopped that thought. He didn't want to get too far ahead of himself.

"Nice job out there, Simon!" Kya said, swimming over. "You'll make the Deep-Sea Divers with me, for sure."

"Thanks," Simon said. "You were great." Then he turned to Cleo. "And you were too. I hope we all make the same team!"

Cleo smiled. "That would be so fun!" She seemed a lot less crabby than her brother.

The sea creatures floated around until, finally, one of the coaches posted a piece of seaweed paper to a coral pole. It was the team lists.

Kya and Simon raced over with the others. But when they got there, Simon was too nervous to look. He covered his eyes and asked Kya to give him the news.

There was a long silence. Then Kya said, "Simon, you made it. We both did." But her voice sounded strange.

Simon uncovered his eyes and checked the lists himself. He gasped. It was true. His name *was* there. But it wasn't on the Deep-Sea Divers list with Kya's. It was on the list for the Tidal Waves!

TIDAL WAVES	DEEP-SEA DIVERS
Bob	Kya
Simon	Elle
Cleo	Leon
Larry	Angie
Nell	Olly

The Divers
vs. the Waves

On the way home, Simon and Kya rode the current in silence. Simon felt terrible. Kya had spent all that time practicing with him and giving him tips so that they could play for the Deep-Sea Divers together. And now he'd made it onto the opposing team! That wasn't part of the plan.

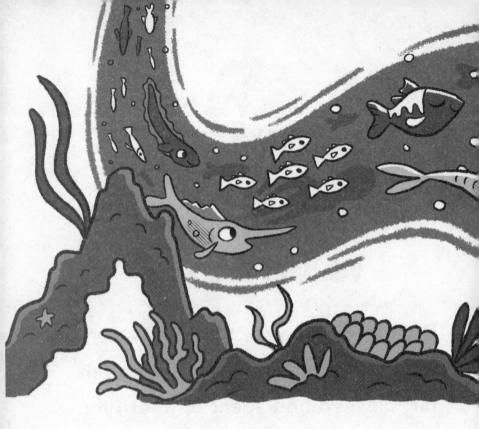

Simon tried to figure out what to say, but nothing seemed right. He wished he knew what Kya was thinking, but she was quiet too. Was she angry with him?

Simon was so worried that he
didn't even remind her about the kelp
ice cream. And Kya seemed to have
forgotten all about it.

When they got home, the whole family was waiting to hear the news. Simon noticed that a few of his siblings were even wearing Deep-Sea Divers headbands to show their support.

"So, did you make it?" Earl asked eagerly.

Simon nodded with a small smile. "Kya and I both did," he said in a soft voice.

His siblings cheered. But Simon noticed Kya was off to the side, quietly putting away her bubble ball gear.

"I'm so proud that both of you are Deep-Sea Divers!" Mr. Seahorse said.

Simon swallowed. "Actually, only Kya is a Diver," he said. "I'll be playing for the Tidal Waves."

Everyone fell silent. They looked at Kya, who only smiled and swam away to her room.

Simon sighed. He wanted to go after her, but he wasn't sure what to say. Should he apologize to his sister? The problem was, Simon wasn't sure exactly what he'd be apologizing for.

Mr. Seahorse swam over and put his fin around Simon's shoulder. "That's great news, Simon," he said. "And a little friendly–or *family*–competition never hurt anyone," he said with a wink.

"Thanks, Dad," Simon said, hoping he was right.

That night, dinner was awkward. Kya seemed to have no trouble chatting and laughing with the rest of the family as she told them about tryouts. But it seemed like she was ignoring Simon the whole time.

After dinner, while they were doing dishes, Simon finally worked up the courage to ask, "Kya, are we okay?" Simon was too nervous to look at her, so he focused on putting plates away instead.

"Sure. We're great!" Kya said. Then she wrung out the dish sponge and swam off to her room without another word.

Simon sighed. No matter what his sister said, things were *not* great between them. And he still wasn't sure why.

7

Practice, Practice, Practice

The next week was filled with bubble ball practice. Every day after school, Simon would pack his bag and head to Seagrass Fields. As he practiced with his team, he saw Kya training with hers. He would wave and she would wave back, but they almost never talked.

And unlike when they went to tryouts together, they always traveled to and from practice alone.

Simon was glad that Cam's sister, Cleo, was on his team, though. It was nice to see a familiar face. Plus, she was a really great bubble ball player.

Simon knew the rules of the game, for the most part, but now he was learning how to play as part of a team. He and the other Tidal Waves

practiced passing the bubble balls to one another. That way, if someone on the other team was coming for your ball, you could hand it off to a teammate who was open.

They practiced helping each other propel forward by creating waves with their fins and tails and claws and tentacles. Then they practiced using those fins and tails and claws and tentacles to block bubble balls.

By the end of the week, Simon was proud of how much he'd improved. He couldn't wait to show off his new skills at the first match that weekend. He only wished he could share it all with Kya.

Finally, the day of the big match arrived.

That morning, Simon and Kya both got ready. They ate and stretched and put on their gear. *If only we could be getting ready together*, Simon thought.

The rest of the family didn't seem to notice that anything was wrong. They were all talking excitedly about the game. They were decked out in hats and headbands for *both* teams: the Deep-Sea Divers *and* the Tidal Waves!

As Simon and Kya packed up their bags in silence, Mr. Seahorse swam over. "No matter what happens today, I'm proud of both of you," he told them.

"Thanks, Dad," Simon and Kya said together. They glanced at each other and then quickly looked away.

"Good luck!" Mr. Seahorse said. "We'll see you at the game."

Simon nodded and followed Kya out the door.

The
Big Game

When Simon and Kya reached the current, Simon hesitated. Should they ride to the match together? Were they allowed to do that if they were on opposing teams?

Finally, Kya said, "Simon, you go ahead without me. I'll just take the next current."

"Um, okay," Simon said. It didn't feel right, but clearly that was what Kya wanted.

As he hopped into the current, his stomach was filled with nerves. Simon was worried about the game, but he was also worried about things with Kya. What would happen if his team won? Or if they lost?

When Simon got to Seagrass Fields, his team was already warming up. He rushed over to join them. A few moments later, he saw Kya hop out of the current and join her team. Too late, Simon realized he hadn't even wished her good luck.

"Are you ready?" Cleo asked him.

Simon nodded. "I think so," he said, but his stomach still felt wobbly.

Honk! The trumpet fish referee blew her trumpet nose to signal that the warmup was over. The match was about to start!

"All right, team," the Tidal Waves coach said. "Let's go out there and make some *waves!*" He chuckled at his joke.

The Tidal Waves let out a cheer, and Simon cheered along with them. He was still nervous, but he couldn't wait to play with his new team.

As Simon swam out onto the field, he tried to find his family in the stands. But there were a lot more sea creatures watching than he had expected. In fact, the stands were nearly full!

Simon gulped and went to take his spot with the rest of his teammates. Cleo flashed him a claws-up, and Simon gave her a good luck fin wave.

Then they waited for the referee to trumpet again and start the game.

Honk!

And they were off!

Simon rushed toward the bubble ball tank to grab his first ball. Then he hurried out onto the field. Around him, players from both teams were swimming around so fast it made Simon a little dizzy.

As Simon swam toward the nearest goal, he spotted Kya charging across the field with her bubble ball. He gasped. She was coming straight at him!

He Shoots, He Scores!

Simon froze as Kya rushed toward him. He watched as she sped right past and hurled her bubble ball into the goal. She scored! It was the first goal of the game!

The crowd went wild. Simon started cheering too. He was so happy for Kya! What a great goal!

Then he suddenly realized . . . he shouldn't be cheering. He should be *playing*.

But it was too late. A lobster from the other team hurried over and popped Simon's bubble ball with his claw. Ugh!

Simon rushed back to get a new bubble ball. This time, he was more determined. He dodged an angelfish and flipped past an octopus. As he spun, he caught a glimpse of Kya scoring another goal.

But Simon stayed focused. The other team's net was in sight. He swam over and shot the ball. His aim was a little off, but luckily Cleo was there to tap the ball in.

Goal!

Simon could hear the crowd cheering, but he didn't stop to enjoy it. Instead, he charged over to a tank to get another bubble ball. But before he got there—

Honk! The referee trumpeted for halftime.

Simon was breathing hard as he swam over to huddle up with his team. He couldn't believe he'd assisted his first goal!

"Great work, Tidal Waves!" the coach said. "It looks like you're having a *ball* out there. And the game is all tied up."

Simon blinked. He'd been so focused on playing, he hadn't been paying attention to the score.

"Just stay focused and the *tide* will turn in our favor," the coach went on, chuckling again.

Simon had to admit he loved a

joke, but not at a time like this. Still, he cheered with his team, eager to get back out onto the field.

As the game started up again, Simon grabbed a bubble ball. He took a deep breath, gathered up all his energy, and swam as fast as he could toward the goal.

He spotted the lobster coming his way again, but this time Simon was ready. He spun up and over the lobster, used his tail to pop the lobster's bubble ball, and then propelled himself forward. It was everything Kya had taught him. Simon raced toward the goal—and scored!

The crowd roared. Simon had never heard such a beautiful sound.

But as he swam toward the bubble tank, the crowd roared again. At the other end of the field, Kya had scored too! Simon knew that meant the game was still tied.

Meanwhile, Simon's teammates were passing a bubble ball down the field. They shot the ball, but were blocked by an eel on the Divers.

Kya was also trying for a goal, but a lionfish on Simon's team used her spikes to pop Kya's ball.

Simon grabbed another bubble ball and was going to head for the goal when suddenly Cleo charged past him and scored!

Honk!

The referee trumpeted the end of the game.

Simon couldn't believe it. His team had won!

Teamwork Makes the Dream Work

Simon's entire team was cheering, and so was the crowd. But if Simon had just won, why didn't he feel happier?

He glanced across the field at Kya, but her back was to him. She had gathered with her team. Her head was down.

Simon sighed and swam over to his team to celebrate. Then the Tidal Waves and the Deep-Sea Divers lined up to shake fins and tails and tentacles.

"Good game," the players told each other as they went down the line.

When Simon got to Kya, the two of them shook fins but didn't say a word. Simon's stomach dropped. He was glad his team had won, but he was worried that Kya was mad at him.

Afterward, Simon's family and friends hurried over to congratulate him.

"You're a natural, Simon," Mr. Seahorse said, pulling him into a giant hug.

"Wow, Simon. I didn't know you could move that fast!" Olive cried.

Even Cam told him, "Good job."

"Thanks!" Simon tried to smile, but his chest still felt tight.

When it was time to head home, Simon turned to find Kya waiting for him. Before she could say anything, Simon hurried over to her.

"I'm sorry," Simon blurted out. "About the game."

"Sorry?" Kya asked. Then she laughed. "Don't worry about that. I've lost plenty of times before. I'm just so proud of you, Simon!"

"You are?" Simon asked surprised. "I thought you were mad at me!"

Kya frowned. "Why would I be mad at you?"

"Because I made it onto the Tidal Waves after you spent all that time helping me practice. I know you wanted us to both play for the Divers."

"Oh, Simon," Kya said. "I'm not mad at all! I'm so happy that you made the team!"

"But . . . you stopped talking to me."

"I didn't want to distract you," Kya explained. "I wanted to make sure you stayed focused on the game and didn't worry about having to play against me."

Oh, Simon thought. *I guess that makes sense.*

"But watch out," Kya teased. "Next time, my team won't go so easy on you."

"We'll see about that," Simon shot back.

They both laughed.

Simon was so relieved. Kya wasn't mad at him. And now that he'd discovered how much he loved bubble ball, he was excited to have a fellow player at home to talk to.

"So," Kya said, "are you ready for that kelp ice cream now?"

"Can we invite both teams to come with us?" Simon asked.

Kya smiled. "Absolutely!"

Simon smiled back. Then the two of them linked tails and went off to celebrate together.

SIMON'S STORY

Once upon a time, many tides ago, there was a seahorse named Simon. He and his sister Kya lived with their family at Coral Castle. Simon and Kya were known for being the best bubble ball players in the whole kingdom. They were so good that they were invited to play in the international bubble ball league and travel around the world: from the Indian Ocean to the Caribbean Sea to the Arctic!

In their biggest match against the Saber-Toothed Tiger Sharks, Simon and Kya did a special move where they created a tidal whirl distraction and then scored the winning goal of the game!

From that day forward, they were celebrated as not just the best players in their kingdom, but the best in the whole world!

Here's a peek at Simon's next big adventure!

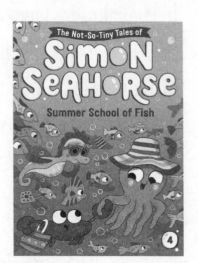

"And that's why the crystal jellyfish glows!" Simon Seahorse said.

The other students in the class cheered. Simon grinned as he swam back to his seat.

Simon had been excited to tell his

An excerpt from *Summer School of Fish*

classmates all about bioluminescent ocean creatures. He wished he could glow with electric light too! And he'd been extra excited about *this* report because it was the last one of the year.

"Nice job," his best friend, Olive Octopus, whispered as Simon sat down next to her.

"Thanks," Simon whispered back.

There was only one report to go. Then it would officially be Simon's favorite time of year: summer vacation. Simon loved school, but there was nothing like the freedom of summer.

An excerpt from *Summer School of Fish*

"Thank you, Simon," Ms. Tuttle said. "Cam, it looks like you're our final presenter."

Simon squirmed in his seat as Cam Crab scuttled to the front of the room. Cam had a tendency to go a little overboard with his reports because he *really* loved facts. And he *really* loved showing everyone how much he knew about certain subjects.

"In my report I will be sharing dozens of fascinating facts about yeti crabs," Cam began.

An excerpt from *Summer School of Fish*